I Love You

Illustrated by Sanja Rescek

Published by Sequoia Children's Publishing,
an imprint of Phoenix International Publications, Inc.

8501 West Higgins Road, Suite 790
Chicago, Illinois 60631

59 Gloucester Place
London W1U 8JJ

Sequoia Children's Publishing and associated logo are trademarks and/or
registered trademarks of Phoenix International Publications, Inc.
© 2018 Phoenix International Publications, Inc.

www.sequoiakidsbooks.com

10 9 8 7 6 5 4 3 2 1

ISBN 978-1-64269-042-2

I love you so much,
and do you know why?

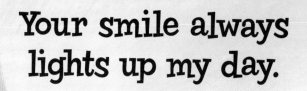

Your smile always lights up my day.

Your eyes sparkle like
the stars in the sky.

You have such a
good, kind heart.

You give the best hugs in
the whole wide world.

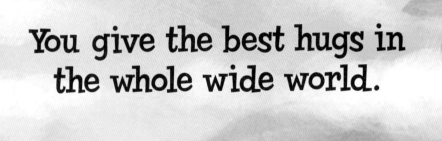

Your laugh is one of my
very favorite sounds.

You make every
moment so special.

I love you so much
because you are the
one and only you!